IMAGINE THAT

Licensed exclusively to Imagine That Publishing Ltd
Tide Mill Way, Woodbridge, Suffolk, IP12 1AP, UK
www.imaginethat.com
Copyright © 2022 Imagine That Group Ltd
All rights reserved
2 4 6 8 9 7 5 3 1
Manufactured in China

Retold by Nancy Lambert
Illustrated by Richard Watson

ISBN 978-1-80105-490-4

A catalogue record for this book is available from the British Library

Heads, Shoulders, Knees and Toes

Retold by
Nancy Lambert

Illustrated by
Richard Watson

Heads, shoulders, knees and toes,

knees and toes.

Heads, shoulders,
knees and toes,

knees and toes.

And eyes ...

and ears ...

and mouth ...

and nose.

Heads, shoulders,
knees and toes,

knees and toes.

Toes, knees and shoulders, head,
shoulders, head.
Toes, knees and shoulders, head,
shoulders, head.

And nose and mouth and ears and eyes.
Toes, knees and shoulders, head,
shoulders, head.

Now start again, but this time
miss out a different body part
each time you sing the rhyme!